Feb 2021

To Dorre[...]
from
Uncle Maurice &
auntie Sandra

GROOTY FLEDERMAUS FINDS A FRIEND
By D.L. Kruse

To the real Grooty Fledermaus
and every child (and adult)
in need of magic and dreams, everywhere.

ISBN 978-1-777-2096-6-7

Through the window nice and wide,
Katie frowned and looked outside.
Kids were playing on the run,
Kicking balls and having fun.

Mom came near and squatted down.
She had seen poor Katie's frown.
"You can't play ball like those kids can,
But never mind – I have a plan."

"A car ride, yes? What do you say?
Gram and Gramps are home today.
The trip is not too far though, is it?
Their farm will be so nice to visit!"

"Oooh yes, Mom!" Katie laughed with glee.
"This trip will be just right for me!
I'll have Gram's cookies – not store-boughten,
And Gramps will say,
'How GROOT you've gotten!'"

Mom laughed and held her daughter tight.
"You know he will, you know you're right!
Your Opa's Dutch and 'Groot' means 'great',
Or 'big', or 'grand' at any rate.

"Take a jacket to stay warm,
The wind is chilly on the farm.
Now let's pack up and out we go,
They love to see you, don't you know!"

Past the houses, fields, and trees,
Such a day to feel the breeze.
Soon in sight they saw the barn,
"That's it! We're here! We're at the farm!"

Gram burst out, her hair in bun,
From the farmhouse on the run.
"Dearest Katie!" Grandma cried,
"You're here to visit! Come inside!"

"Katie, Sweetheart!" Gramps yelled out,
"How groot you've grown! I had no doubt!
I see you're dressed up nice and warm,
Let's take a toodle 'round the farm."

"I'll lift your chair out right away,
I'll set you in it, then we'll play!
The house can wait, the day is warm,
Let's you and me explore the farm!"

With Katie settled in her chair,
Gramps pushed her down the path to where
The barn stood tall and big and red.
"A surprise inside!" her Grandpa said.

And there, inside a nest of hay,
A batch of little kittens lay.
Their furry mother kept them warm,
Kept them close and free from harm.

Then Katie saw a little bump –
The hay! It jiggled, then it jumped!
And two green eyes and two BIG ears
Slowly from the hay appeared.

"My goodness gracious! What is that?
Could it be? Why yes! A bat!"
But then, another thin stick rose –
What the heck? It had some toes!

Gramps and Katie peered so close
And then they saw a tiny nose,
A tiny face, a ribcage too,
A scrawny tail came into view.

What is this? What is that?
It looked to be part bat, part cat!
It shook, it shivered, its skin was bare –
Oh my gosh, it had no hair!

"Oh Grandpa, look! Please bring him near.
He's just so little, I want him here."
Katie held him, hands so warm,
But Grandpa spoke up with alarm.

"He's way too thin, he's not been fed,
I'm so surprised he's not yet dead.
He has no hair, yet still alive,
But winter's coming, he'll not survive...."

Then Katie heard a rumbling sound,
Soft and low. She looked around.
"Oh, hear that Gramps? He's purring now!
He trusts me Gramps! I don't know how.
I want to take him home with me,
He'll be alright at home, you'll see!"

"Well, ask your mother, she might say no....
It's the weirdest thing, no hair to grow.
Those ears too big, those eyes too green,
He's the strangest kitten I've ever seen!

"Four little legs and those ears like a bat.
Big round tummy but tail like a rat.
So many parts and none the same,
Hmmm...
He's quite a mess, but he'll need a name....

"He's strong in spirit
Though he's small as a mouse
So perhaps you could call him...

"Grooty Fledermaus!"

When Mom saw Grooty, she looked surprised
But she saw the joy in Katie's eyes.
So late that night, when tucked in bed,
Katie smiled at Groot and then she said,

"You're hairless yes, but here's the catch,
Without my hat, we're both a match.
The doctors say my hair will grow,
And so might yours, you never know."

And Grooty purred and touched her cheek,
And with that touch, she heard him speak.
"We're different, yes, but special too.
Together there's so much we'll do."

Katie, sleepy as could be,
Showed no surprise at all that she
Could understand him – every word!
His message she had clearly heard.

Grooty yawned and stretched, and then he said,
"This is a very comfy bed!
So go to sleep now, my new friend,
The sweetest dreams to you I'll send.

"At night, in sleep, in dreams we'll fly,
We'll see the world, just you and I,
And while you sleep, we'll travel far,
Sometimes past the nearest star."

And Katie sighed, now fast asleep
So Grooty made not one more peep.
But Grooty purred because he knew...

That everything...was purr-fect.

Thank you so much for purchasing Grooty's book
and sharing the incredible world of
childhood imagination and magic.

If Grooty's story has entertained you and your
child and lifted your spirits even just a little bit,
Grooty and I would be honored if you would be
so kind as to leave a short review on Amazon
or Goodreads or any other reading platform.

-Much love from us both,
D.L. Kruse and Grooty Fledermaus

Follow Grooty and Katie in their
magical adventures together!

- Grooty Fledermaus and the Troll's Tears (Book Two)
- Grooty Fledermaus and the Dragon's Dream (Book Three)
- Grooty Fledermaus and the Unicorn's Horn (Book Four)
- Grooty Fledermaus and the Mermaid's Magic (Book Five)
- Grooty Fledermaus and the White Whisker (Book Six)
- Grooty Fledermaus and Grandpa's Gift (Book Seven)

Manufactured by Amazon.ca
Bolton, ON